8/18

Finn Finds a Friend

Written by Jenna Grodzicki

Illustrated by Alexis St. John

WEST HARTFORD · PUBLIC LIBRARY

D1362050

To Shawn. Thank you for your never-ending love and support. - J.G.

Finn Finds a Friend

Copyright © 2017 by Jenna Grodzicki

Artwork Copyright © 2017 By Alexis St. John

All rights reserved. No part of this book may be reproduced in any form or by any electronic or mechanical means including information storage and retrieval systems – except in the case of brief quotations embodied in critical articles or reviews – without permission in writing from its publisher, Clear Fork Publishing.

Summary: Finn is not your typical lemon shark. He likes to frolic and have fun in the water. But his brothers' and sisters' idea of fun is lying completely still on the ocean floor - BORING! While out searching for new friends, Finn encounters a sea turtle who hides in a rock cave. Clearly, he must want to play hide and seek. Then he comes across some humans who scream, "SHARK!!!" when he approaches. Obviously, they must be excited to see him. Will Finn ever find a friend who can see beyond his sharky appearance?

PJJ
GRODZICKI
JENNA

Clear Fork Publishing

P.O. Box 870

102 S. Swenson

Stamford, Texas 79553

(325)773-5550

www.clearforkpublishing.com

Printed and Bound in the United States of America.

Hard Cover ISBN - 9781946101440

Soft Cover ISBN - 9781946101495

LCN - 2018938537

SPORK

Life was boring at the bottom of the ocean.

Finn wiggled and waggled back and forth, trying to convince his brothers and sisters to play with him. Like most lemon sharks, his brother and sister pups spent their days laying completely still on the ocean floor, their flat heads and broad snouts camouflaging them in the sand.

Not Finn. He blew bubbles. He swam upside down.
He counted barnacles. But it was no fun playing by himself.

One early morning,
Finn went in search of a friend.

He hadn't swum very far when he came across a creature wearing a shell!

He swam up to the animal.
"I'm Finn! Would you like to play with me?"

The turtle darted into a nearby rock cave.
"Hide and seek!" said Finn. "I love that game!"

Finn swam through weeds. He nosed behind boulders. He wriggled into the rock cave.
Until finally...

"I found you. You can come out now!"

"No way! I don't want to be shark food!"
called the turtle.
"But I'm not here to eat you. I just want to *play*."
The turtle peeked out. "Not taking any chances,"
he said, before disappearing into the cave again.

Disappointed, Finn swam on.

He came across some strange animals swimming
and splashing. They didn't have tails or fins like his,
but they were making friendly sounds

Pasting on his brightest smile, he sped toward the creatures.

As he got closer, a scream pierced the air and
he heard cries of, **"Shark!"**

They're happy to see me, Finn thought.

The closer Finn got, the faster they swam away.
"This is awesome," said Finn. "They want to play tag."

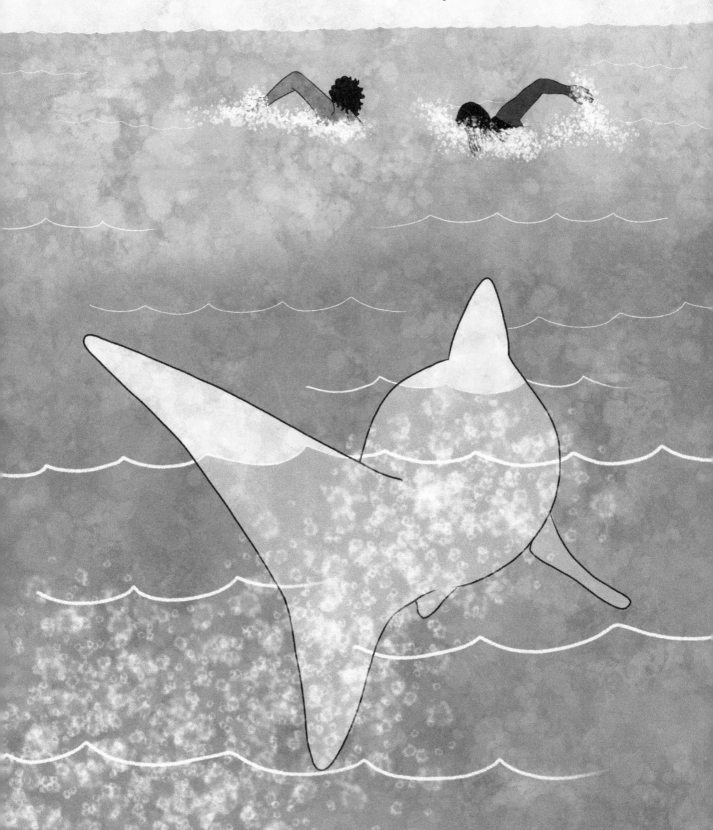

Soon, a loud WHIRRING noise filled the air,
and waves rocked Finn back and forth.

"Where did they go? Didn't they understand
that I just wanted to play tag?

"I'm not giving up," vowed Finn.
But finding a friend who could see
past his sharky appearance
was harder than
he thought.

His smile drooped.
His fins sagged.

Finn continued swimming
until two creatures diving
in and out of the water
caught his attention.

One more chance,
Finn thought.

"Hi, I'm Finn. Would you like to be my friend?"

"You're a shark!" the larger one replied.
"We can't be friends with you! Echo, let's go!"

Finn turned around, ready to glide home. He hadn't gotten very far when he heard a cry from behind.

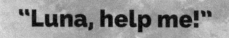

"Luna, help me!"

Echo's tail was
tangled in seaweed!
Finn had an idea.

"I can help."

He swam up to
Echo,teeth bared.

"He's going
to eat me!"
she shrieked.

"Wow, you weren't going to eat me, you were trying to help."

"Thank you for saving my sister."

We know that now. I'm Luna. This is my sister Echo."

"You're welcome. I was looking for someone to play with, not eat."

"It's nice to meet you. Would you ike to play?"

"Sure. What do lemon sharks like to do?"

Finn smiled. "Probably the same things that you like to do."

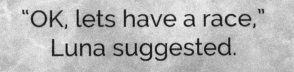

"OK, lets have a race,"
Luna suggested.

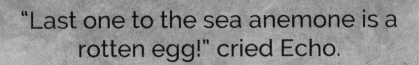

"Last one to the sea anemone is a
rotten egg!" cried Echo.

Finn hurried after his new
pals, his heart flipping.
He had a whole list of games
they could play next.

Finn's story is fiction, but lemon sharks are real. They may look scary, but they're not considered dangerous to people. They mostly eat bony fish, mollusks, and crustaceans. Dolphins are not on their menu! And no, lemon sharks do NOT eat lemons!

Lemon Shark Fast Facts

- Lemon sharks get their name because of their pale yellow coloring.
- Lemon sharks live primarily in shallow waters near the shore.
- They can be found in the Atlantic Ocean, the Pacific Ocean, and the Gulf of Mexico.
- The mother lemon shark gives birth to a litter of live babies, called pups. Each litter may consist of 4 – 17 pups.
- The pups live in an area close to the shore called a nursery. They live in the nursery for several years before swimming out into deeper waters. This is to protect them from predators.
- Young lemon sharks lose an entire set of teeth, one at a time, every 7-8 days.
- Adult lemon sharks can grow to be 8 – 10 feet long and can live for up to 30 years.
- Due to their closeness to the shore, it is not uncommon for lemon sharks to be seen by swimmers and surfers. In fact, lemon sharks will sometimes gather in groups around docks.

Still interested in learning more about lemon sharks?
Your local library can help you find great information. Here are a few other resources to get you started.

- Florida Museum: https://www.floridamuseum.ufl.edu/fish/discover/species-profiles/negaprion-brevirostris/
- BBC Nature: http://www.bbc.co.uk/nature/life/Lemon_shark
- National Geographic: https://news.nationalgeographic.com/news/2013/12/131206-lemon-sharks-return-birthplace-homing-bahamas-science/
- SoftSchools.com: http://www.softschools.com/facts/animals/lemon_shark_facts/475/

Jenna Grodzicki
Author

Jenna lives in Connecticut with her husband, two crazy awesome kids, a cat named Pixie, and a dog named Ozzy. She has a Bachelor's Degree in Elementary Education from Boston College and a Master's in Education from the University of New England. Her first book, PIXIE'S ADVENTURE, was awarded two Honorable Mentions in the 2017 Purple Dragonfly Book Awards. She recently traded in her librarian hat to become a full time writer. At all hours of the day (and night) she can be found at her desk, drinking iced coffee and working on her next story. When she's not writing or spending time with her family, Jenna LOVES to read! She also enjoys skiing and cheering for the best team in baseball, the Boston Red Sox.

Alexis St. John
Illustrator

Alexis St. John spent the first part of her professional life as a fine artist. Her work was shown in galleries across North America and the Caribbean. The paintings featured unique characters and worlds, and she was often asked to tell stories about the paintings. Alexis started developing these worlds and writing stories about the characters until one day she realized she had become an author and illustrator. Alexis spends her days illustrating and creating worlds in her studio near Seattle, Washington.
website: alexisstjohn.com

CPSIA information can be obtained
at www.ICGtesting.com
Printed in the USA
BVHW02s1313150818
524606BV00014B/135/P